Mayhem and Mystery at the Kitty Kastle

by

Malynda McCarrick

Mayhem and Mystery at the Kitty Kastle

Copyright © 2014 by Malynda McCarrick

Cover Art by Rebecca K. Sterling of Sterling Design Studios

All rights reserved. Except for use in any review, the reproduction or utilization of this work in whole or in part in any form by any electronic, mechanical or other means, now known or hereafter invented, including xerography, photocopying and recording, or in any information storage or retrieval system, is forbidden without the written permission of the publisher, Malynda McCarrick.

This is a work of fiction. Names, characters, places and incidents are either the product of the author's imagination or are used fictitiously, and any resemblance to actual persons, living or dead, business establishments, events or locales is entirely coincidental.

Malynda loves to hear from her readers and fans. You can contact her at www.malyndamccarrick.com or find her on Facebook.

I dedicate this book to the tireless workers at *The Cat House* in Lincoln, Nebraska

Learn more about the work they do at: www.thecathouse.org

Prologue

"I think we've covered everything you want. I'll get the estimate to you by Friday and, if you decide to go ahead with the renovations, we can get the work started by next week."

Miranda Bailey took the card the contractor handed her and walked him to the door. Jay Carpenter came highly recommended and she was pretty sure he'd be doing the work they required to get the building renovated and customized to suit their unique needs. Playing hard to get was just good business, she didn't want to look too eager...even though she was. She told herself the eagerness was for the shelter's new living arrangements, but she suspected she had reasons beyond that. Jay Carpenter, hunkiness in a tool belt and those eyes! She heard of the rare condition where a person's eyes could be two different colors, but on him it was electrifying. One eye green and the other eye split down the middle with one half green and the other half brown. She knew this because she couldn't help but get a closer look. She was up in his face and only realized it when she was gently, but firmly, set away from him with his strong hands on her upper arms and an irritated look on that handsome face.

"Great. I'll look it over, present it to the Board, and let you know what we decide." Miranda stood in the front doorway of the building and watched as Jay got in his pickup truck and drove away. The "Board" consisted of herself and a handful of volunteers who ran the cat shelter but Jay didn't need to know that. Their small band of workers had their work cut out for them as soon as the shelter was relocated from the small building they currently occupied to this larger location, a historical old warehouse-type building that was donated by one of their anonymous supporters. The building had been sitting vacant for the past year while lawyers handled the paperwork necessary to transfer ownership to the shelter and its many feline occupants. The property was now listed as belonging to Miranda and the non-profit under the name of the *Kitty Kastle* and they were ready to do business.

Miranda couldn't wait to move in. It was early May and they had several seasonal, warm months to work on the building before the Midwest winter would set in.

They had three floors to renovate. How long would it take to renovate? She'd soon find out. It was easy to change their name to the *Kitty Kastle*, the new location really promised to be the castle of her dreams.

Meanwhile, she had wonderful news to share with her counterparts back at the shelter's current location. The building had been donated but they still had many years of fundraisers ahead of them to be able to furnish the place as needed.

But...oh, what fun they had to look forward to!

Chapter One

"Where do you want the desk to go?" Miranda looked up from the pile of boxes on the floor of her office and found Kaye, the shelter director, and two of their volunteers, Emmy and Carson, waiting for her to make a decision.

"Oh. Well. I guess over there, facing the door. I can always move it later." She absentmindedly swung one hand in the general direction behind her and dug back in to the boxes. This was her favorite room of the new shelter, the study. She was the only one who called it that, though. The others just used such terms as "den" or "family room" but keeping with the age of the majestic old building, Miranda felt it needed a "study." It would serve as her office. With built in bookcases along three sides of the room, she looked forward to filling those shelves with several years of books she'd collected at the old shelter, mostly novels and classics but there were a few cat oriented reference books that always came in handy, too. When she'd hired the contractor to do the renovations, the one luxury she needed for herself was this office, complete with those newly constructed floor-to-ceiling bookcases.

The building, which had at one time been broken up into apartments and lofts, brought with it a few furnishings, things left behind by previous occupants but nothing of any value. Its ownership had been tied up in legal mumbo-jumbo but there were no heirs waiting to lay claim to anything, as far as she knew.

Acquiring the building at this particular time had worked out perfectly for Miranda. Her messy divorce found her homeless and unable to afford a new home. She was moving in upstairs – on the third floor of the shelter, to be exact – and what meager belongings she was able to load into the freight elevator and haul upstairs were safely stacked in boxes in one of the bedrooms and waiting for her to unpack. Everything else from her former life stayed behind with the ex-husband and she wouldn't miss them...neither the material goods nor the ex-husband.

This would be a new beginning and a new life for her as well as the cats. In the front hallway they were moving in and their hisses, growls and angry voices echoed throughout the spacious front entryway.

"Minx got out of her carrier again...ornery little lady." The sleek black cat, Minx, joined them in the office as though she hadn't just outwitted her carrier and escaped from the army of volunteers hauling carrier after carrier in and dropping them off in one of the back rooms. The plan was to park them in one room until everyone was unloaded and accounted for then the task of releasing them to explore their new home would follow. Minx was never one to wait for humans to make her decisions, she had a will of her own and was already establishing who was boss in their new home.

"That's okay, just let her explore," Miranda stopped Carson when he would have scooped up the cat. "She can't get into much trouble, everything is still in boxes so there's nothing for her to get into."

"Sure, okay," Carson agreed. "I think we've brought everything in that goes in here. I'll go help unload the other rooms." He and Emmy left together, leaving Miranda alone with Kaye.

"So, what do you think?"

"About what?" Miranda asked.

"Well...let's start with your new home. How do you like your new home?"

How did she like her new home? What a silly question. "What's not to love? It's a *Kastle*, right?"

"Are you sure this is what you want? Or are you just using this as a place to hide out from the real world...as usual." Kaye had always been a little too perceptive for Miranda's comfort. This was one of those times but that didn't mean Miranda had to give in so easily.

"I don't know what you're talking about. What would I have to hide from? Besides, this place and these cats need me. Living here just makes sense. The place is big enough for the cats and me...plenty big, in fact, for anyone else who might choose to live here." Yeah, she was hiding out.

"Okay. I give up...for now. So. Where do you want me to dig in?" Miranda let out the breath she had been holding, relieved that Kaye was changing the subject...for now.

"How about you check in with the volunteers and make sure the kitchen is stocked and organized. I'll figure out what needs our attention after that. Once those kitties are released, they're going to be hungry."

"Good plan."

Miranda watched her friend leave while a subtle sense of longing ached in her chest as she thought about what would happen later that night. She would be alone...with a big hollow warehouse full of cats. All other humans would be home with their families.

She would be alone.

Chapter Two

It was an enormous task that she had taken on, renovating and repurposing a huge old warehouse and taking residence in one of the bedrooms upstairs. Jay Carpenter was well acquainted with the cat rescue shelter who had hired him, but not the woman who was in charge of it.

Jay was more of a dog lover than a lover of cats but any animal deserved to be treated well. The *Kitty Kastle* earned his respect for the hard work they put into giving all those cats a good life but that didn't explain why he'd taken the job. It wasn't about money, he had plenty of that. His business was never short of money, his tumultuous childhood had taught him how important it was to make money and create security in his life, and that's what he did. This project went beyond the money, it was about taking care of creatures that couldn't take care of themselves. If he could be a part of that, he was all in.

It took over two months to get the building in good enough shape for them to move in but it would take a couple of years or more before the place was completely renovated. Miranda made it clear from the beginning that they planned to make improvements as money was available. The mechanicals were highest priority. The basic structure was in surprisingly good shape so they would not need to waste much time or money there.

They moved in yesterday and the first call came in this morning. Miranda was having problems with the electricity, it sounded like she was blowing fuses and needed him to come out and check it out. His guess was they were overloading circuits or trying to use appliances that were not compatible with the building's old circuitry. Maybe this would convince her to get that wiring updated sooner than planned.

That was why he was on his way to the *Kitty Kastle* at eight o'clock in the morning.

When he pulled up in front of the shelter, Miranda greeted him at the door.

"I don't know what happened, one minute everything is fine then the whole shelter went dark. Do you think we blew a fuse or something?"

He snagged his tool belt and fastened it around his waist as he followed her inside. "I'll have a look at it and we'll find out. Where were you when it happened?"

"Upstairs in the master bathroom." The master bathroom was nothing more than a bathroom located near the bedroom she had fixed up to be her own. The building was too old to have original indoor plumbing so an actual "master suite" was a recent addition, left over from one of the apartments the renovation process had obliterated. Her need to label it in modern terms was nothing short of amusing.

He followed her up the long staircase to the third floor, avoiding the slow moving freight elevator, but knew they would find nothing there. "Right in here." Yep, the bathroom. "I was drying my hair and...see? Dead." What caught his attention more than the hairdryer was the black cat staring back at him from its perch on the pedestal sink. A precarious seat but the cat seemed firmly planted. And those eyes... "Oh, that's Minx. Don't mind her, she's claimed this place as her own. She's probably checking you out to see if you are worthy." Miranda chuckled a little at that and he could only guess it was an inside joke. He didn't get it.

"You need a GFI in here."

"Yeah, I remember you saying something about that in the original quote."

"You really need a GFI in here."

"We can't afford any more changes right now. Maybe when—"

"I know…when you have some money coming in. I need to go check the circuit box in the basement, but I know what I am going to find. While I do that, why don't you think about that GFI and we can talk about ways we can help you afford it. How's that?"

"Okay, but—"

"I'll go check the breakers and meet you downstairs." He didn't stick around to hear any more arguments. For this building to be a safe place for Miranda and her shelter they were going to have to find a way to update that wiring now instead of later. If he had to do it no charge, that's what he'd do. Later he would figure out why he felt compelled to provide a safe home for this particular woman and her weird collection of cats.

Three flights of stairs and he was in the basement and heading for the fuse box. He thought he was alone but when he heard a noise behind him on the stairs, he turned to find that black cat, her eyes on him, monitoring his every move. Why something as ridiculous as one little cat would seem significant to the moment, confused the normally rational man.

It was just a cat.

But it was more.

Then he surprised himself.

"What do you want? Don't you trust me down here by myself? You can trust me. What trouble could I get into down here, or what do you think I would possibly be interested in...I can't believe I'm talking to a cat." He was rewarded with a deliberate cocking of the cat's head to the side and a slow blink of those glowing yellow eyes and what looked suspiciously like a smile.

He turned back to the fuse box and checked everything inside, clicking the breakers where needed and closing the door of the cabinet when he was done. Then he turned back to the cat.

But the cat was no longer sitting on the stairs.

"Here, kitty, kitty kitty..." Again, he felt ridiculous talking to the cat but couldn't seem to stop himself.

"Meow."

Not usually a jumpy person, when the cat spoke to him from the floor at his feet he was startled enough to drop his flashlight, sending the cat running off to a dark corner away from him. Had the cat been hit by the heavy flashlight? Was she hurt?

"Here, kitty, kitty, kitty..."

"Meow."

He picked up his flashlight and followed the sound of the voice. She was sitting in one of the few bare spots, the only place not filled with piles of furniture or boxes.

"Meow."

"There you are. Are you hurt?" Again, he wondered why he spent so much time pursuing the cat. He was a dog person...right?

"Meow."

As he drew near, the cat rose to her feet and walked away from him, the short distance to the wall behind her, then sat facing the wall. He swept the beam of his flashlight over her and she swung her head to look at him, then swung it back to face the wall. When he was close enough, he knelt down to get a look at the cat. She seemed uninjured. Then she raised one front paw and started scratching at the wall in front of her. What he thought was a concrete or brick wall, now appeared to be some sort of paneling or plywood. A wood paneled wall in the basement?

Under closer inspection, it proved to be a carefully constructed wooden wall, complete with molded panels and sealed seams. At some point in time during the life of the building, a skilled carpenter had been down here and built a wooden wall over what Jay guessed was a brick foundation wall. Why? Did somebody live down here? Was this another apartment?

He reached toward it to check it out.

"There you are. I was waiting for you upstairs. Did you find what you needed down here?" Miranda's voice jerked him from his thoughts and the cat disappeared while he rose to his feet.

"Yeah, sorry. I fixed the breakers you need. Let's head on upstairs and talk about the long term repairs I think you should consider."

"I don't have the money—"

"We can work something out." They talked as they climbed the stairs together then closed the basement door at the top.

Chapter Three

Miranda worked out a deal where Jay would be kept on as their handyman but she wasn't sure how she'd managed it. The first job they needed him to work on was the wiring. He agreed to update the wiring throughout the entire building. A major task, one she would never have been able to afford on the shelter's budget. What he wanted in return for the work remained a mystery. He told her he wanted nothing but when did a man not expect something in return for something? She decided she had no other choice but to accept his help, the consequences of trusting him...well, she would deal with that later. Would it be such a hardship to...give in...to the man if he asked? He was certainly attractive enough and good with his hands, but what about the man as a person? Would he just turn out to be like her ex? And why was she thinking about stuff like that?

"Everybody seems to be settling in nicely. We even got a glimpse of the elusive Spaz. That's better than we got at the old shelter." Carson, the shelter's volunteer newsletter editor joined Miranda in the large kitchen at the back of the shelter. Something they were very specific about when they thought through the reconstruction process, they needed a massive kitchen containing multiple refrigerators for the various medicines and specialty foods their resident cats would need.

Spaz was the calico everyone knew would be the cat who would have the toughest time adjusting to the move to the new location. They suspected that the poor girl had suffered abuse at the hands of her previous owner. She was elusive, yes, but Miranda knew she had her mushy, cuddly moments at night when they were alone in her apartment on the third floor. Miranda decided not to embarrass the kitty by telling anyone else their little secret, though.

"She'll be fine she's just going to take a little longer than the others." The "others" being the hundred or so kitties freely roaming the three floors of the new shelter.

"Oh, and before I forget to tell you...Felix and Archie were playing with something weird. I thought it was one of the new toys the volunteers put together for the garage sale, but when I really looked at it I couldn't tell where it came from. Did you give them some new toys I haven't seen yet?" Miranda leaned back on the counter and sipped at her breakfast smoothie, not really concerned about the mystery toy but curiosity made her ask since every detail of the shelter was supposed to be pre-approved by the shelter's president.

"What did it look like? I think you've seen everything we have," Miranda asked.

"Some kind of crocheted yarn ball. The way they were playing with it I'm guessing there was catnip inside."

"No. I can't think of any yarn toys we have available. I will check it out and make sure it's nothing left over from previous tenants that may need to be disinfected or thrown away. Where did you see them playing with it?"

"In the playroom." The playroom, the largest single room in the building designed for the cats to engage in play without damaging any furnishings. When Miranda saw a similar room in a cat specialty magazine, she knew they had to have one at this new location. Jay worked his magic in creating the room just from the pictures she had provided. The space was opened up to one large empty room then Jay built various climbing structures and tunnels for the cats to explore and enjoy. It made Miranda – almost – wish she were a cat. It turned out even better than the pictures in the magazine and she'd swear Jay even enjoyed creating it. Again, she had to wonder what was wrong with the man. He seemed like the perfect man, but why was he working here and why was he so hard to figure out? Shaking it off she realized Carson was still standing there waiting for a response.

"Okay. I'll check it out."

"I'm sure it's nothing to worry about, but...you know. Those boys have come a long way in their healing and it would be awful if they got in to anything in their new home that made them sick again."

"My thoughts exactly," Miranda said then set her empty glass in the sink and went looking for the cats in the playroom. Located on the first floor, like the kitchen, it was just down the hallway and past her office.

Sure enough, the two were there playing with a crocheted yarn toy. When she reached for it to get a good look, Felix snatched it away with a possessive growl and trotted away to a corner of the room then turned to look at her, a look of satisfaction on his face. While she waited for him to lose interest, Miranda took a moment to look around the cat-customized room.

All four walls had ledges and cubby-holes for the cats to climb, play in, and hide from the others. Varying levels of padded condos were cleverly located along the trail of ledges lining the walls with occasional perches here and there so the cats could rest or scope out the other cats while playing, running, or stalking their playmates.

Genius. Jay did a fabulous job and the cats were showing their appreciation every day, enjoying the kitty jungle gym.

Looking back at Felix, Miranda found him looking away from the toy and she snagged it before he could stop her. What she found was a Twinkie shaped hand-crocheted toy, obviously created with skill and attention to detail. Three things about the toy surprised and disturbed her, though: the toy looked brand new, it was not one that had been made through any of the *Kitty Kastle's* usual sources, and the toy had Felix's name embroidered on its long side.

"Carson!" she shouted out the door, hoping to catch the volunteer before he left for the day. "Can you come to the play room for a minute, please?" But it wasn't Carson who popped his head in the open doorway.

"Carson went home. What do you need, can I help?" Daisy, one of the other volunteers, asked.

"Oh. Sorry. Yes, maybe you can." Daisy was one of two volunteers whose main responsibility was to feed, clean and count cats each day. A daily inventory was vital in keeping track of their resident cats, especially while they were still settling in to their new location. If anyone knew where the cats had been spending time – or where they would have found the mystery toy in Miranda's hand – Daisy would be that person. "Do you know where this toy came from?"

"Hmm, let's see." Miranda handed it to the other woman and watched as she looked it over then handed it back. "Nope, I have no idea. It's not one of ours. Why?"

"That's just it...I'm wondering where it came from. It looks new but unless we know it's clean and safe, I think we need to quarantine it. Maybe it's just coincidence that *Felix* is embroidered on it."

"Hmm, maybe. I didn't notice that. Heck of a coincidence that Felix has a toy with his name on it, though."

"That's what I was thinking. Here," Miranda handed it back to Daisy. "Can you put it in a plastic bag and stash it in one of the microwaves until I get a chance to nuke it? Better safe than sorry, and Felix really seems to like it so if we can give it back to him, he will be happy. We want our boy to be happy, right?"

"Yeah, the little sweetie." Daisy reached down to scratch Felix across the back then took the toy from Miranda and left the room.

"Oh, and, Daisy?" Miranda halted her before she got out the door. "I'll be in my office working on some promos for the garage sale and kitty cabaret. I should have something for Carson to put in the newsletter by this evening if you want to check with me later."

"Sure thing." She left Miranda alone with her thoughts, the least of which was the origin of the mysterious kitty toy. Beyond the toy, her mind still worried over how they were going to pay for the electrical updates Jay was already working on.

But worrying never got a person anywhere. Redirecting her brain, she headed for her office and the stack of paperwork she knew awaited her there. It would be a long night of event planning and brainstorming for future events. Being a non-profit meant non-stop fundraisers and coming up with unique events was one of her favorite tasks at the shelter.

Chapter Four

Most of the time, Jay worked independently on the jobs who hired him. It cut down on expenses and made scheduling a lot easier and more efficient. Unfortunately, this job required him to hire a couple of extra hands to get it done. He would be paying for the help from his own pocket since he had agreed to do the work for free. Updating the electrical at the *Kitty Kastle* shelter was turning out to be a bigger job than he had anticipated.

He was in the attic, if the building were actually a house. It was technically the fourth floor, the one above where he had built the apartment for Miranda on the third floor. This floor had shorter ceilings so he had to duck to get around. He was stringing wire for the lighting on the floor below him, checking supporting fixtures around where he would hang ceiling fans, and ripping out all the old wiring. The sweat running down his back and face reminded him this was the only floor they had decided not to include in the air conditioning plan. It was his one suggestion for saving money and time in the renovations and he was sure wishing they had gone with the air conditioning.

As he installed the wiring in one hole then strung it across the floor to the next outlet, he bumped up against the wall. It was mere inches from the fixture he was wiring and seemed to be an exterior wall but something did not seem right.

If he remembered correctly, the ceiling fixture on the room below was more than four feet from the exterior wall. So why was the wall set so far in on this level? It did not make sense. A few inches difference, maybe, but a few *feet* was a huge discrepancy, even considering the slant of the ceiling that was almost enough room for a full hallway.

A secret hallway?

Jay reached for the wall with his hammer and lightly rapped. Twenty inches to the left then twenty inches to the right. He located wall studs in the right places, hollow spaces in between those studs. Hollow, not insulated or backed by an exterior wall. Hollow.

"Hey, Jay. We are going to head into town for pizza. You with us?" One of his workers, Wade, popped his head in the room where Jay was working. Startled, he spun to face him, his back bumping the wall behind him and he felt the hammer catch on something.

"Uh, no...thanks. I need to finish here before taking a break. You go ahead." Jay waited until he heard the other man's footsteps on the stairs before turning to check on his hammer. Just what he had dreaded, he had punched the hammer through the wall and when he bent to pull the hammer free, he pulled a good chunk of sheetrock out with it. A hole the size of his fist was left behind.

Easy enough to fix but aggravating just the same. As he stepped back to inspect the damage, a beam of light flashed at him through the hole then quickly disappeared.

"Meow." Startled for the second time in the last short minute, he spun around to find that darn black cat sitting there looking at him.

"Meow."

"What do you want, Cat?" *Talking to cats, Carpenter? Have you lost your mind?* "I don't know about you, Cat, but I've got work to do so if you don't mind...beat it."

And the cat surprised him by flicking its tail at him and turning to leave, passing through the same doorway Wade had just exited, then disappearing without another look back at Jay.

With a quick look at his watch, Jay figured he had less than an hour before he had to be somewhere, so he got back to work. If he had time later, he told himself, he'd try to remember and repair the hole in the wall, maybe follow up on the wall placement, too.

Not now, though. He had a load of supplies being delivered on another job and if the truck was on schedule he needed to be there.

Chapter Five

"Um, Miranda? I think you need to see this..." Daisy popped her head in the doorway of Miranda's office, jerking Miranda from nearly dozing off at her laptop. "It's playtime in the playroom and you're not going to believe what I found when I just checked on our kitties there."

"Why don't you just go ahead and tell me, I'm in the middle of...oh, I don't know what." If she were being honest she'd admit she'd been only seconds away from a much needed nap at her desk.

"No, I think you need to come and see," Daisy insisted.

"Okay, maybe the walk will do me good."

"Yeah, like I said, you're not going to believe this." Intrigued, tired, but with curiosity outweighing fatigue, she got up from her desk and followed Daisy to the playroom. What she initially found when she got there was a crowd of volunteers milling about in the doorway, but they parted to let her in when she approached. "There. Look."

There were at least twenty of their resident cats playing independently around the room, in corners, on ledges, under furniture, and some just planted in the middle of the room. The apparent reason they were independently playing had to be the toys they each focused on, each cat with its own toy. Handmade, crocheted toys in a variety of colors and designs.

"Are those...?"

"Yes, just like the one Felix was playing with and each one has their name embroidered on it. Personalized and customized for each cat." Stunned, Miranda stood watching the cats play, oblivious of the humans watching them. "What do you want us to do...I'm assuming you want us to do something...right?"

"What? Oh...no. Nothing. Wait...yes. Gather everyone in the conference room as soon as possible. We need to figure out where these are coming from.

Somebody here has to be supplying them, I just want to know who."

Daisy hurried off and the rest of the volunteers slowly turned to follow, Miranda assumed they were heading to the conference room for the impromptu meeting. Miranda was left watching the cats play and trying to calm the twirling questions rolling around in her head. Who was making these toys and secretly giving them to the cats, and why were they not admitting to such a sweet generous act?

* * * * *

"You can wipe those frightened looks off your faces this meeting isn't going to hurt. I promise." Miranda looked around the circle of people she had come to think of as friends and family. Each person knew their job responsibilities and there were no slouches amongst them. "We appear to have a mysterious benefactor who is gifting some of the resident kitties with their own, handcrafted, personalized toys. While I have no problem with the kitties having these toys, I am curious to whom we give credit for the contribution. So, that's the reason for this hastily organized meeting."

A wave of relieved whispers flowed over the group then quieted as Miranda waited for somebody, anybody, to speak up and take credit for the generous gifts. Other than seeing confused scans pass from one person to the next, the group remained silent then focused all eyes back on their leader.

"Nobody is in trouble. Really. I just want to give credit where credit is due." Silence. Then the group of equally curious and confused cat lovers jumped in unison as the sound of a loud mechanical "meow" announced a visitor at the front door. "But first order of business…we are disconnecting that recording as our doorbell," Miranda told the group. "It creeps the heck out of me every time it sounds." A few giggles eased the tension in the room as the group dispersed and Kaye headed for the front door to see who had set off the annoying doorbell.

"So the mystery remains…" Miranda muttered to herself on her way to her office.

Chapter Six

He didn't know whose dumb idea it was to install the gimmicky doorbell but was glad they made the decision to have it disconnected. When he hit the button and heard the obnoxious noise sounding from inside, he seriously considered walking away even though he was there to work. Miranda told him to just let himself in but since the place was her personal residence as well as a business, he was not comfortable making himself that…comfortable.

Today he was loaded down with catalogs of commercial fixtures. He and Miranda were still in disagreement on how much work he should be doing at this point but he considered himself the winner in the battle since the building was basically non functional in terms of electricity, as far as he was concerned. They were lucky the building had passed inspection but that inspection was based on reassurances that work was still in progress. It helped that he was able to call in a few favors with the city inspector, too.

Miranda was thumbing through the last catalog behind that ridiculously huge desk of hers as he sat impatient in the chair facing her across the cluttered surface of the desk. The black cat sat perched on the corner of the desk glaring at him, daring him to speak or move. He uncrossed and re-crossed his legs for the tenth time and leaned forward in his chair, gearing up to speak.

She beat him to it.

"I don't know. These are all very nice but…" Money. That's what made her hesitate.

"Which are you leaning toward?"

"They all look so…fancy." Yes, she meant expensive but he guessed she was too proud to say it.

"If it's price you're worried about, don't be. I get contract prices on everything."

"I don't know. I am not very good at this. Why don't you just pick something out and go ahead with it." He didn't know what surprised him more, the woman agreeing to go ahead or that she was trusting him to make the decisions. Then she gave herself away. She rubbed at the sides of her head with both hands, pain visible on her beautiful face. This woman, he suspected, was a bit of a control freak but he had to give her credit for all the work she did around the place. It couldn't be easy running a non-profit organization, splitting your time between taking care of the animals under your care but also coming up with new ways to raise money.

"Look, why don't I just pick out what works best and get to work. You have enough on your hands here and I have some ideas about what this place needs." He didn't, but he had a lot of work ahead of him and was anxious to get at it.

"Yes. Yes, that sounds good. I just…"

"I'll get right on it and let you know." He rose from his chair and gathered up the books, tucking them under one arm as he headed for the door. "Trust me."

After hauling the books out and dumping them in his truck, he let himself back in with tool belt strapped in place and toolbox in hand, ready to get back to work on the attic room. He stepped on the freight elevator and let it take him to the fourth floor, its creaky grinding gears a reminder of how much work still needed to be done on the old building and its parts.

Right now, though, there was an attic wall that still did not make sense to him and he intended to get answers today.

Chapter Seven

It was Friday, bill paying day, and Miranda sat at her desk staring at her computer monitor with another headache forming between her eyes. Always a meticulous financial wizard, what stared back at her was what had caused the headache. One hand reached for the intercom installed on her desk, hitting the button blindly, afraid to take her eyes from the screen in front of her.

"Kaye, can you come in here, please?"

"Sure, I'll be right there." Seconds later footsteps announced Kaye as she entered the office. "What's up, Miranda?"

"Um, I'm not sure…" Miranda waved the other woman to join her behind the desk. "I guess I just need somebody to tell me I'm not imagining things. What do you see here?"

"Well, let's see. It looks like…holy crap! Is that our bank account?"

"Yes. Yes it is. What do you see?"

"Where did all that money come from?"

"Oh, so you are reading it the same way I am. My eyes aren't playing tricks on me?"

"No, Miranda. We have a butt load of money in our account. Is it a mistake? Did the bank screw something up?"

"No, they say it's correct. Somebody has been depositing money in our account anonymously, ten thousand dollars at a time. Anonymous. Do we know anyone named Anonymous?" Lame joke, she knew it as soon as the words left her mouth, but Miranda was having a tough time with what she was seeing. Sure, Kaye snickered at the pun but shock may have been a factor.

"How long has this been going on?"

"If we can trust the transaction history, it looks like at least a month. Then, this week this deposit for fifty thousand appeared. Fifty thousand dollars! Who has that kind of money to anonymously deposit into our account and how does somebody go about depositing money into somebody else's account without them knowing about it?"

"I don't know, the owner of the bank, maybe…"

"Get serious! I'm freaking out a little here! What if it's dirty money somebody is hiding in our account? We don't know where it came from, maybe some Nigerian scammers or something hacked into our account!"

"Hackers take money *out* of your bank account, they don't typically put money *in*. Anyway, we are a non-profit, isn't that how we had the account set up? I don't think I'd complain too much about somebody wanting to give us money without us having to campaign or beg for it."

"Maybe they are hiding it from the authorities there, maybe the Government will come after us thinking…oh, I don't know…whatever!"

"Calm down, Miranda. Let's think this through. You've already talked to the bank and they say it's legit?"

"I don't know about legit, they just confirmed it wasn't a mistake."

"So, if they say it isn't a mistake they must know who has been making the deposits, wouldn't you think? I mean...they aren't going to do anything that could be traced back to a mistake they might have made."

"Yeah, I guess that makes sense. But..."

"No buts. Accept the money and be happy."

Accept free money without questioning it or worrying over its source? How could she do that?

"But..."

"I said no buts. Now, what should we spend the money on?" Kaye, always good at finding ways to spend money. But Miranda was grateful for the money – if it turned out to really be honest money from a good donor – and grateful that she had Kaye by her side. "I say we put more money into the building. What projects did we put off because of money?"

Miranda would have said the electrical updates but those were being covered by Jay. What other projects were worth over sixty-thousand dollars?

"Maybe we should just leave it in the bank for future expenses, at least until we're sure the money is ours to spend."

"Fuddy duddy. You're no fun sometimes," Kaye pouted but the pout did not last and soon her smile was back in place. One of the many things Miranda loved about her long time friend and employee, nothing ever got her down and she seemed able to keep that positive attitude in place no matter what. A modern day hippie, Kaye didn't care what other people thought of her and her casual wardrobe advertised what a free spirit she was. "Maybe we could spend a little on the kitties, get them more condos built in the play room?"

"I'll think about it."

"Couldn't you suggest it to the Board?" An inside joke, Kaye knew they were basically the only Board members.

"Goofball."

"Yeah, but you still love me," Kaye tossed over her shoulder as she left the room, her small victory in tow. She knew Miranda would spend the money when given the option to spoil the cats.

Chapter Eight

Back in the attic, Jay finished installing the wiring needed on the new lights for the third floor and settled back to rest a minute and think about the mystery wall in front of him.

The hole he had accidentally punched stared back at him, daring him to look inside. He was still trying to convince himself that the light he had seen earlier was just his imagination.

Maybe it was a light from downstairs, filtering up through the wall. If that were the case, he'd need to chase it down and fill whatever hole was allowing light through. If there was not a hole...

No.

No way was somebody behind that wall with a flashlight.

It sure would explain the placement of the wall, though. With the wall at least four feet in from where it should be – flush with the outside wall – there actually could be space enough for a small room or passageway behind that wall.

But why? Why would there be a passageway hidden behind that wall?

No. Utter nonsense. No way was there a hidden passageway, his imagination was just getting the better of him.

But what if...?

Then another thought hit him.

"Hey, Wade," he called to the footsteps he heard approaching from the hallway. When he got no answer, he tried again. "Wade?" No answer, so he checked out in the hallway to see where the other man was. The hallway was empty. He was sure he heard footsteps out there, clear as day. At least he thought the sound of footsteps was coming from the hallway.

Then they sounded again. Quieter this time but definitely footsteps and the sound was not coming from the hallway.

Turning back to the hole in the wall he'd just been examining, the footsteps echoed then stopped as suddenly as they'd started.

Jay had never been a superstitious man, nor was he scared by unexplained phenomenon found in old buildings, but that did not stop the shiver that raced down his spine.

"Meow." The shiver turned to a near heart attack when his favorite black cat appeared at his feet.

"Shit, Cat! You scared the crap out of me!" *Talking to a cat again, Carpenter?*

"Meow."

Then Jay noticed something hanging from the cat's mouth so he reached down to get a closer look.

Hanging from a red ribbon, tightly gripped between the cat's teeth, was a skeleton key. Not a shiny new key, it was old, well worn and used. When the cat lowered her head and let the key drop to the floor, Jay snatched it up.

His mind raced over every door in the building, trying to picture any lock that would accommodate a skeleton key. He came up blank. All current doors were new or replaced in the last twenty years or so, nothing was original to the centuries old building. Nothing that he was aware of, anyway.

Where would the cat have picked up an old skeleton key...which was strung with a new piece of red satin ribbon?

"Where did you get this?" *Again. Talking to a cat, Carpenter?*

"Meow."

What did he expect, that a cat would open up and tell him all about the key and where she got it? Then the cat surprised him...again...for the second time in the last five minutes. She walked over to the hole in the wall, stretched up on her back legs, and reached one of her front paws inside, batting at the hole as though playing with somebody on the other side.

Jay didn't get a chance to check it out, his cell phone rang and the mood was broken.

"Yeah, Carpenter here." He watched the cat as he took the call then picked up his toolbox and turned to leave the room. "I can be there in a half hour. Do you know where the shutoff valve is? Good, good. Turn it all the way off and I'll be there as soon as I can."

He turned one last time to see what the cat was up to, the key still gripped in his hand, and found her sitting in the same spot facing him.

He would swear the cat was smiling at him.

Chapter Nine

"We just got something delivered. I had them leave it in the foyer until you had time to open it…it's really big," Kaye announced as Miranda was putting away the books to go looking for something to eat.

"What is it?"

"Um, we won't know until you open it. I know how much you love surprises so we left it for you to open. Come on. It's up front." Miranda could tell Kaye was anxious to see what had been delivered, they hadn't ordered anything so Miranda guessed it had been delivered to them by mistake.

When they reached the front foyer, Miranda found most of the shelter's workers checking out the package as though it was Christmas morning. She could not blame them, the package was bigger than she was and there were no clues to what was inside.

No return address, no identifying marks on the box and no packing list attached.

"What are you waiting for? Hurry up! Open it!" One of the volunteers was dancing from foot to foot with anticipation, the same look Miranda saw on everybody's face.

She ripped into the package, just as anxious and curious as each person in the group gathered around her. The yards of nylon strapping fell away, staples popped out at the hand of her screwdriver and pliers, then the cardboard. She was left with something encased in Styrofoam. The Styrofoam ripped easily away to reveal something she had just two days ago been shopping for online in her office: a full sized heated massage table for the cats. When she saw it online she imagined how much comfort and joy it would bring the older and less healthy felines in their shelter. A table shaped bed, the size of a twin bed for humans, with built in remote controlled heat and massage.

"But I..." The words didn't reach her mouth...the mouth that hung open in shock and surprise.

"Weren't you just telling me the other day how cool it would be to have one of these?" Kaye asked.

"I decided the money could be better spent on sensible stuff, like food and medicines. I don't know where this came from."

"But yet, here it is."

Yes, it was.

Their mysterious benefactor had struck again, but this time Miranda was left feeling a little more than anxious about their gift. She had been shopping online for this. Other than showing it to Kaye, she had not spoken a word about it to anyone.

"Kaye, I need you to come with me to my office. Everyone else, please get back to work. And...will somebody please move this somewhere out of the way until I figure out what to do with it?" Miranda didn't wait to see if her orders were followed, she just knew she needed to get to her office. The one and only place the massage table had been discussed.

Why did she feel like she had been spied upon and why was she so scared by that information? Because her office was her inner sanctum and now the privacy and security she counted on had been taken from her.

"What's up, Miranda?" Kaye followed her into the office and they closed the door behind them. "What's with the top secret meeting suddenly?"

"Who else did you tell about that massage table? Who knew I was looking at it?"

"Nobody."

"You didn't tell anybody? Nobody at all?"

"No, I really haven't had time and I didn't think it was important since you decided not to get one. Why?"

"The massage table that was just delivered. You aren't the least bit curious who sent it and how they knew I had been looking at them? Not at all curious?"

"Uh…coincidence?"

"Mighty big coincidence, if you ask me. No, it feels like…do you think there could be a bug in here?"

"Bugs? What kind of bugs, I thought we had the place exterminated."

"Not bugs, *a* bug. You know…like a listening device?"

"Now you are sounding paranoid. Why would anyone want to bug you? That stuff only happens on TV and in the movies."

"Yeah, I know. But…shh, somebody's coming." Miranda knew she was acting ridiculous over something that should make her happy, but if somebody had been spying on her to learn of the massage table what else did they know and why would they spy on her? She was just the founder and CEO of a local cat shelter not international intrigue or homeland security issues. Why did she feel violated, vulnerable, and stalked? Shouldn't she be happy that they were getting the shelter's needs fulfilled without spending any money?

A knock on the office door announced that they had company.

"Come in," Miranda said without bothering to ask who it was. Jay and one of his workers, Wade, entered the room.

"The lights on the third floor are done. Check it out when you get the chance and let me know what you think," Jay said, then shot a look at Wade. "We'll be working in the basement today, getting that main power box updated and installed. Is there anything else you needed before we head down there?"

"No. I can't think of anything," Miranda said then a thought hit her. "Do you know anything about surveillance devices?"

"A little bit. Why, you want a security system installed? Might be a smart idea. We can do that."

"No…I mean yes, that might be a good idea. But I was asking because…um…would you be able to detect a bug if it were…say…hidden in this room?" She could tell that she had surprised him, his silence and the look he sent her way spoke volumes. He thought she was crazy. Yeah, as soon as the words left her mouth she wished she could take them back.

"With today's technology, there are thousands of different cameras that could easily go undetected, some are tiny and you wouldn't even notice them. Is there a reason you think there's a bug in here?" Then she realized where his mind was going.

"I don't think you put anything in here, if that's what you're thinking. No, it's just that…well…something odd happened and I am having trouble finding an explanation for it." The two men exchanged another look then turned back to her to elaborate.

"Sheesh, Miranda. Just tell them," Kaye piped up. "She thinks somebody is spying on her because we received a massage table today that she'd wanted and the only way they would have known she wanted it was if they had been listening in on a conversation we had here in her office two days ago."

"Coincidence?" Wade asked and Jay remained silent, his eyes roaming over the room.

"Mighty big coincidence," Kaye copied her words.

"Yes, I guess it is. Jay? What do you think? Could this room be bugged for some reason?" When he didn't get an answer, he asked again. "Jay?"

"What…oh…yeah. I guess anything is possible," Jay answered but his eyes were still wandering.

"Earth to Jay…"

"What? Oh," Jay snapped back to attention but to Miranda he still seemed distracted. Did he believe her, that there was a bug somewhere in the room? "I was just…anyway. We'll be in the basement if you need us."

Jay turned to leave and Wade followed him, after an apologetic shrug to Kaye and Miranda.

"That was weird," Kaye voiced what Miranda was thinking.

"Yeah, it was almost as though he was mentally trying to figure out where there would be bugs hidden in this room. Do you believe me, now? If Jay does, don't you think it's possible?"

"I didn't say it was impossible, I just don't see why anyone would want to do it, that's all."

Chapter Ten

"Are you going to tell me the real reason why we are working in the basement? That box was replaced three days ago and is working just fine," Wade started in on Jay as soon as they made it to the bottom of the basement stairs, keeping his voice low so he would not be overheard. "And do you believe somebody is bugging her office?"

"I have something to tell you and it's going to sound crazy but…"

"Yeah, I know. Something weird is going on here. I've noticed it myself."

"You have? What weird stuff have you noticed?"

"You mean besides you?" Wade joked. "Plenty."

"Like what?"

"I'd swear sometimes that I hear people walking around behind the walls. That's crazy...right?" Jay chose not to answer right away. "Jay? That's crazy...right?"

"Yeah...no...I mean, I hear it, too. I heard it upstairs, when I was working in the attic. But there's more. I thought I actually saw a light behind the wall."

"How would you see a light behind a wall?"

"I accidentally punched a hole in the wall, up there in the attic. When I was working up there I know I saw something like the beam of a flashlight moving around then it went dark."

"How can that be?"

"That's what we are down here to find out. Here, take a look at this wall." Jay steered Wade towards the wall by the power box, the wall in front of where he had first met that black cat.

"What exactly am I looking at?" When Jay just pointed, Wade leaned in and got a better look. "Looks like paneling. What is so strange about that? Lots of people finish their basements with paneling."

"It's not paneling. It looks more like a wall, not just something covering a wall."

"Huh?"

"Here, let me show you what I mean." Jay pushed by Wade to put himself in front of the wall then reached out and knocked on it. "Hear that? There is no foundation wall behind that. I think this is a wall constructed to block off another room."

"There's an easy way to find out, why don't we just tear it down?" Jay had already considered that but work on other areas of the building had been keeping him busy. He was not currently busy, and he had Wade to help, so now they were going to check it out.

"My thoughts exactly. Did you bring your crow bar?"

"Don't leave home without it," Wade joked and pulled the tool from his tool belt at the same time Jay located his own, then they both stepped up to the mysterious wall. "Where do you want to start? Do we just rip into it or are we trying to save it to reinstall once we've checked out what's behind it?"

"No rules. If we can save it, sure, but if not…"

"What's the boss lady going to say about you ripping walls down without her okay?"

"She's never been down here and I doubt she ever would be. You know women, spiders and dirty cellars are better left to the men." Wade snickered a little at Jay's obviously sexist remark but did not disagree with the logic.

Both put their crow bars at opposite sides of the panel of wood and together they pulled. The wood screeched in protest at being disturbed, then gave way easily, pulling away from its frame and opening up to reveal a black void of open space. There was no wall behind it.

"What the hell…" Wade said what Jay was thinking.

They pulled the panel completely free from the frame and leaned it on the wall beside them, out of the way, then peered into the dark space they'd just revealed.

"You bring a flashlight?"

"No. You?"

"I might have one in the truck. Hold on, I'll go get it." Wade quickly ran up the stairs taking two stairs at a time while Jay stood staring into the dark hole, trying to make sense of it. He ran one hand over the frame of the opening, one that had been carefully crafted, not just two-by-fours thrown in as a frame to nail a board to. This looked like a doorway or a planned wall instead of what they'd first guessed it was, plywood nailed over a spot in a crumbling foundation.

Then something else hit him.

He walked around the perimeter of the foundation, eyeing where it met the joists and sill plates of the floor above them. Again something seemed odd about the placement of things.

"Here, I had a couple." Wade returned and handed Jay one of his large contractor grade flashlights. "What are you looking at now?"

"Does something seem odd to you, where the first floor should meet the foundation."

"No, not really. Looks like everything is where it should be. Why, what do you see?"

"Here, about five feet in." Even though they were standing near the overhead lights, Jay pointed the beam of his flashlight where he wanted Wade to focus his attention. "What does that look like to you?"

"Looks like there's a wall anchored there, but then…the outside wall is there. What the hell?" Jay watched Wade scratch his head as he walked back and forth between the two places where the wall seemed to be located. Jay had already checked it out a couple of times in the past few days, so he knew where they would find the interior walls upstairs. The protruding screws poking through the floor above them clearly outlined each room on the first floor. Rooms located at least five feet in from the exterior walls of the building. "You know what I think?"

"If you think that the previous owners built secret walls, rooms and passageways around the perimeter of the building, then yes I know what you think."

"Damn, looks like we have us a mystery on our hands, here. Do you think we'd find anything downtown to tell us if any permits were filed for the original work when they did it?"

"My guess is that the permits wouldn't show this. Yeah…we have a mystery on our hands."

"Let's take a look at what we uncovered behind that wall." Wade did not wait for Jay's okay, he pointed his flashlight into the dark hole and walked in, leaving Jay behind.

"Hey, wait up!"

Chapter Eleven

Miranda climbed out of bed the next morning after a long night of tossing and turning. Every creak and groan of the old building seemed magnified since yesterday's activities.

After she shook off the feeling of being stalked, she decided it wasn't worth worrying about. They had a new massage table and there were dozens of older cats that could really use it, so they set it up and gave it a try.

One cat after another tried it out, with very little coaxing from the humans. They just plugged it in adjusted the motion and heat then introduced one cat. Soon the bed was covered in lazy, contented, but comfortable kitties.

It was worth it. Having the bed give comfort to arthritic and disabled kitties made accepting the anonymous gift worthwhile.

So why could she not relax?

Too many good reasons, tens of thousands of reasons, cash that wasn't theirs yet actually was. Even though they had a hefty balance in the bank account, each time Miranda thought of some way to spend it she didn't get the chance. Jay was covering the electrical updates, the massage table appeared at their front door with no bill or strings attached. Their refrigerators were full of kitty food, enough to last them for the next year…just another mysterious delivery that appeared on their doorstop this morning.

All these things should have made Miranda happy, ecstatic even, but she was experiencing the opposite. She wasn't confused or bewildered, she was scared. Her past made her cautious, it was also that past that rekindled the fear. Could a person be stalked by a good Samaritan? Was she being overly dramatic? Maybe. Maybe not.

Then there was the night filled with bumps, groans, and knocks that kept her up. Since she moved into her third floor bedroom she'd enjoyed nights of the best sleep she'd had in her life. She left her door open and several kitties took advantage of it and shared the queen size bed with her. Maybe it was the kitty companions, maybe it was the fact that she worked herself to the point of exhaustion each day, whatever it was she'd slept well.

Until last night.

Last night the moans and groans of the old building went on all night. She gave up trying to sleep at three in the morning. The noises did not keep the kitties from sleeping, just Miranda.

She could not identify where the noises were coming from. It wasn't a howling wind from outside and there were no trees close enough to the building to be brushing against it or scraping a window. The noises seemed to be coming from inside the building, the floor above her and somewhere on the third floor where she lived.

At first she thought she was imagining things, a whisper soft footstep, a person moving quietly down a dark hallway. But the cats heard it, too, their ears perked up with heads tilted, listening to the sound then settling back into sleep when the noise stopped. Miranda wished she could settle back into sleep as easily as the cats did, but no, she lay awake worrying about intruders all night. Intruders or rodents living within the walls of her new home? Wouldn't the cats alert her if there were mice or rats that were shuffling around in her walls?

A knock on the open door of her office yanked her from her thoughts and she looked up to find Jay Carpenter standing there, hesitating before entering her office.

"Do you have a minute?" he asked.

"Yeah, sure. Come on in." She hoped he wasn't there to deliver more bad news, even though they now had the money to cover any new repairs or update needed, she still hated spending the money. Jay walked across the room to the spare chair in front of her desk and dropped his body into it, exhaustion in his posture and on his face. Then Miranda realized that Wade was standing just inside the doorway so she waved him in, too. "Please don't tell me bad news, I don't think I could stand it if I got bad news today."

"I'm not sure if it is bad news or not. I don't think so. I just have something to show you downstairs, in the basement." He didn't wait to see if she followed, he just got up and followed Wade down the hall and toward the basement stairs. Miranda was close behind.

As they started the descent down the stairs, Jay said over his shoulder, "We ran across a wall that looked suspicious so we pulled it down. In these old buildings, people sometimes cover a bad foundation with paneling so they can sell the building without prospective buyers being any the wiser about a crumbling basement wall." Miranda did not care if Jay had to tear down a wall in the basement, she trusted him not to do any damage to her building that he couldn't repair.

"It's back here, behind the stairs. Come take a look."

Miranda followed Jay and Wade to the back of the basement where they had big shop lights set up on the floor, aimed toward what looked like a big hole or doorway in the back wall.

"What am I looking at?" Miranda asked Jay.

"You mean besides a big hole in the wall? Well, I brought you down here to show you what we found inside," Jay said. "This was hidden behind a wooden panel that we removed when we suspected it was hiding a bad foundation. Thankfully your foundation looks in great shape all the way around." Miranda let out the long breath she'd been holding. A room hidden behind a wooden panel? Was it hidden or just forgotten about? "Come inside and see what we found."

She stepped over the piece of wood still lying across the entrance and left the brightness of the shop lights as she entered the room. Jay hit a light switch on the wall behind her and they were drenched in bright commercial light, plentiful fixtures of fluorescent lights lining the finished ceiling leaving no corner of the room dark. This was a professionally designed room, meant for important business to take place and it was built recently.

"Until we knocked down that wall, this room was built to be climate controlled, with moisture barriers and safe from any kind of pests. It looks like a high end storage unit, probably why it was hidden away down here in the basement."

It was then that Miranda noticed the file cabinets and storage shelves filled with boxes and carefully labeled, each label perfectly placed and meticulously identified. The room had to measure at least a hundred foot square, not large enough to be a commercial storage unit but plenty big to store somebody's personal papers and important items. Her fingers itched to look inside one of the boxes or open a file cabinet drawer but something held her back. This was somebody's secret room, all these items carefully stored here were special enough for somebody to tuck them away from prying eyes and secure them in this custom built room.

"Have you looked at anything, just out of curiosity?" she asked Jay, then noticed Wade had left them alone. The lights went out in the outer room and she realized he was packing up the shop lights as Jay showed her the secret room.

"No, it's not my place. I just wanted you to be aware of what we found, it's up to you to decide what you want to do with it."

"But...aren't you even a little bit curious?"

"Are you kidding? Of course I'm curious," he chuckled a little at that but quickly recovered. "But I have a job to do..."

"Nonsense. I would appreciate the help, if you're interested in checking it out."

"Sure. I have always loved a mystery, and frankly this place has left me guessing from day one. Finding this room...well, it's just frosting on the cake."

"What do you mean?" With everything that had been happening since she'd moved into the place, was there more that she did not even know about?

"Oh, nothing. Forget I said anything."

"No, please. What do you mean? What kind of mystery?"

"Have you noticed anything strange about the place, anything happening that you can't explain or figure out? Noises you can't explain?" Did she want to tell him, would he believe her or think she was crazy? The fact that he was asking made her think he would, believe her that is.

"Maybe. Some little things that I can't find an explanation for. Yes." When he did not give her one of those this-woman-must-be-crazy looks, she continued. "At first it was strange things happening in the shelter, anonymous gifts and other stuff like that. Then..."

"Then?"

"Then I started hearing stuff. I thought it was just paranoia on my part, because of everything else, but..." she trailed off, unable to come up with the best way to explain the noises or do it in a way that made sense.

"Let me guess, is it like you hear somebody walking but there's nobody there?"

"Yes!"

"Anything else?"

"The gifts bother me the most. It is like somebody is spying on us, on me, so they know exactly what we need or want and then it mysteriously appears. Can you imagine how that could bother me?"

"Ah, so that's why you were asking about the surveillance devices in your office?"

"Yes."

"Okay, okay. Interesting..."

"Now it's your turn, what have you been noticing?" she asked, if she were sitting down she'd be on the edge of her seat right now. As it was, she found herself leaning toward him, waiting to hear something that would make her feel less…crazy.

"How about discovering this room, for starters?"

"Okay, what else?"

"Walls located where they shouldn't be, a foundation that doesn't line up with the rest of the building, noises that I can't explain."

"Noises, like the footsteps and nobody is there?"

"It's more than that. When I'm up on the fourth floor I should hear noises from the outside, the wind or when there was a thunderstorm the other day.

If the building has the standard depth allowed for insulation, you would still be able to hear wind howling at the walls, especially in a building as old as this. This baby, though, is almost soundproof."

"What do you think would account for that?"

"This is going to sound crazy but you wouldn't hear outside noise if you are in an interior room, one at the center of the building and not located against an exterior wall. It's almost like your building is located inside another building."

"But, that doesn't make sense."

"No kidding." His tone would have come across as sarcastic or biting if she did not suspect a gnawing aggravation was coloring his words. This situation was bugging him as much as it was scaring her.

"So what do we do now?" she asked. She really needed him to be the hero, if ever she thought she could count on another person, especially a man, she needed this man to be her hero.

"I tell you what, why don't I do a little more digging around here and find out what I can about the structure of this building. Do I have your permission to, maybe, dig behind a wall or two for answers, as long as I fix what I've torn down?"

"Absolutely, I need answers."

"Good. Then while I am doing that, you can dig into what we have here and see what you can find. Maybe start with the file cabinets. File cabinets usually hold paperwork, and where there's paperwork maybe there should be answers."

"Sounds like a good plan."

"Oh, and…maybe we should keep this just between us until we get more answers. We don't know what's going on so we don't know who might be behind it."

"But I tell Kaye everything, she's been my closest friend since…"

"Just for now. I'm not saying forever, just until we get some answers."

"Okay. I can do that. Just you and me." She liked the sound of that for some reason. She decided not to question her reasons, just accept it.

"Good girl. Now, I will head back upstairs and talk to you later. Hopefully, this won't take long to get to the bottom of things. We'll probably find that it was all just weird circumstance and the quirks of an old building."

Just what she'd been telling herself earlier.

Why didn't she believe it?

Chapter Twelve

Miranda waited until after Kaye left for the day. If she were to keep the secret of the basement room between her and Jay she'd have to do her snooping when Kaye wasn't around to ask questions.

She grabbed a light snack on the way as she hurried down to the mysterious room in the basement, heavy duty flashlight in hand even though the room was equipped with plenty of overhead lighting. Somehow having her own light source made her feel in control and less vulnerable in case those lights failed. It was bad enough that she would be down there alone, being alone in the dark was unthinkable.

When she reached the opening to the room she felt around on the wall for the light switch and bathed the room in bright light before entering, refusing to acknowledge that the light was what gave her the confidence to continue. Four steps into the room she stopped, letting her gaze wander over the shelves of neatly stacked and organized boxes and the file cabinets lined up like soldiers against the wall facing her. A mental eenie-meenie-mynie-mo placed her in front of the first filing cabinet and she pulled open the top drawer.

What she found inside did *not* surprise her. It was full of unmarked hanging file folders stuffed full of newspaper clippings in various stages of yellowing age and decay. What *did* surprise her was that for all the attention somebody had put into creating this airtight room to store these items, they had not bothered to place the papers in acid-free page protectors or other folders that would have prevented any damage. Unless they had been stored there before such archival products had been invented.

She pulled out the first hanging file folder, opened it flat across the top of the drawer and unfolded the article on top. It was dated over fifty years ago and the picture at the top of the page bore a strong resemblance to her very building.

It was her building, as it must have looked over fifty years ago.

The article was about a grand opening ceremony for the building. A line of people stood in front of the building and they were posing with a large pair of scissors, a ribbon cutting ceremony. Miranda read the description beneath the picture and it identified the people in front, none of the names seemed familiar to her so she read on.

The renovation of the building, dividing it into several rental units, was part of a revitalization project in the area and the owners of the building – Cloris and Dodd Meriweather – were proud to welcome the City Council members to the celebration of the completion of the project. Their piece of the project, anyway. The rest of the project had yet to be completed, pending funding for the building neighboring hers.

Miranda finished the article but did not see anything regarding the goals of the other buildings to complete their part of the renovation project. Those same buildings were currently vacant and looked like they had been that way for a long time, though well maintained they were boarded up and empty. One of the reasons she was happy to move the shelter to the area had been because there were no occupied buildings nearby, leaving them room to expand the shelter at some point in the future.

She flipped the article over and moved on to the next one in the folder.

Again, her building was pictured but several years had passed. This time the picture panned out and she could see the neighboring buildings. In the years that had passed since the last article it did not look like any progress had been made on the other buildings. Though she had not seen any pictures in the first article, the mention of their stalled progress led her to believe something had kept it from happening and the appearance suggested the buildings had been abandoned.

She skipped reading the article and moved on to the next. Another article picturing her building, several years later. As she flipped through the folder she found more articles, at various dates, all about her building.

Curious, Miranda flipped through the rest of the folders in the drawer. All the folders contained newspaper clippings and the last one contained articles just about the couple identified as the owners, Cloris and Dodd Meriweather.

Miranda pulled that folder from the drawer and settled into a comfortable position on the floor to read through it.

* * * * *

Turning over the last article, Miranda closed the folder and set it on the floor beside her, suddenly feeling the effects of sitting in one position for too long. She stretched her legs out in front of her and arched her back into a long stretch of torso and shoulders, her arms reaching over her head and her joints crackling with the effort. She checked her watch and realized that not only had several hours passed but it was after five in the morning. She'd been up all night. No wonder her stomach was protesting and her body screamed with fatigue.

She rubbed her tired eyes as she rose from her position on the floor, grabbing the drawer handles of the file cabinet to pull herself up. Standing with both hands at her back, arching into another body wakening stretch, she let the yawn take over for a second before shaking it off.

All her hours of reading had been informative but she was not sure they were any closer to understanding what was going on around the place. The people she was reading about were strangers to her. She had lived in this city all her life and she'd never heard of anyone by the name of Meriweather, yet the people in the articles seemed to be prestigious citizens of the community. What ever happened to them? The articles in the files she had read so far dated up to ten years ago then they stopped. Had the news stopped becoming important enough to save or had something happened to the person who had been collecting them?

One night reading old newspaper clippings had not answered Miranda's questions it only created more. She needed to find out more about the building she now called home and learn more about the people who used to own it.

First thing in the morning, this morning, after she caught a nap, she was heading to the courthouse to get information on the history of her building. She would have started online, but she doubted she would find anything of great detail there. A trip to the county records department and assessor's office would give her more.

Maybe somebody working there would be familiar with the Meriweather name or their descendents.

Chapter Thirteen

That damned cat was following him around again. It did not matter where he was working, she managed to find him and stalk him. It was not like he was afraid of her, quite the contrary. It was just a little unnerving, being stalked by a cat. A black cat. A black cat with piercing eyes that followed his every move and seemed to be judging him.

Jay thought he had gotten past it. A life where he felt constantly judged, but here he was being judged by no less than an insignificant cat. The cat knew nothing about his past, a life for a young boy being passed from home to home, not knowing love and doubting that love was something he would ever experience in his life.

Given up as a baby, Jay was told that he was abandoned at the hospital by a mother who could not keep him. No more information than that. He grew up not caring, at least he thought he didn't care. So why was he thinking about it now?

Is that why he chose to work at the *Kitty Kastle*? This cat, as well as the hundred or so others being sheltered here, were familiar with abandonment and identity issues. Jay could relate to that. Suddenly he felt a certain level of kinship with the cat who now rubbed against his shins, it was as though she knew what he was thinking and rewarding him for reaching the correct conclusion, discovering their innate connection.

He kneeled down and scratched the cat behind her ears and she rewarded him by starting up her purr machine. Yes, there was something about this cat. Just something.

They were in the attic room again, he and the cat. Keeping true to his vow to Miranda, he was going to look behind that wall and see what secrets lay hidden there. Pulling his hammer from his tool belt, Jay walked toward the hole in the wall with the intent of ripping it a little bigger. Big enough to poke his head in there and look around.

That was his intent.

His forward progress was slowed by the cat. Each step he took she wound herself between his feet, almost as though she was trying to trip him and slow him down. The closer he got to the wall, the more determined she was to halt his progress. When he stood two feet away from the hole he paused and looked down at the cat.

"What are you doing, Cat? Do you want to play? I can't play right now, I'm working."

"Meow."

"I'm busy, get out of the way and let me get by."

"Meow."

Jay stepped over the cat and moved toward the wall, when his foot hit the floor the cat launched herself at him, sinking her teeth into his ankle and catching him by surprise. He stumbled and fell backward, away from the wall and narrowly missed the cat. When he recovered enough to look around it was to find the cat sitting in front of the wall, positioned beneath the hole, in a sentry position.

Guarding the wall, a low growl was aimed at Jay when he moved to stand.

"What the hell...?"

A growl and feral hiss warned him to keep his distance.

He gathered himself and stood but took a step backward, eyeing the cat as he did. And the cat surprised him yet again. She sent him a slow blink of her eyes and purred...loudly. He took a step toward her, the purr turned to a growl. He stepped back, she purred. One more step back and he'd swear he could see a smile on the damn cat's face.

"Son of a…"

"Meow."

He could easily have kicked the cat out of the way and continue what he was doing, but something stopped him. Besides his aversion to abusing an animal – any animal – he had a weird feeling that he just was not meant to look behind that wall. At least not right now. So, now he was taking orders from a cat.

When the cat rose from her spot by the wall and walked out of the room, Jay found himself following her.

He followed her down three flights of stairs and into Miranda's office. That's where the cat jumped up on the desk, turned, and faced him. When she was satisfied that he was paying attention, she extended one of her front paws and started digging at a pile of papers on the desk, her actions knocking them on the floor and making a mess of Miranda's neat and tidy work space. Jay just stood and watched with no thought of interrupting her. The whole scenario felt like a dream sequence from which he could not wake.

Then she stopped. She sat, tucking her tail around her body and the purring began. One paw went out and landed on the only papers left on the desk.

Jay snapped out of the strange trance she held over him and looked at the papers she'd dumped on the floor then to the papers she'd left on the desk. A stack of file folders full of newspaper clippings were on the floor. Left on the desk looked more like something from a tabloid.

"What are you doing in my office?" Miranda said from behind him, and for the second time in the last ten minutes his heart skipped a beat.

"Miranda," his hand went to his chest, trying to calm the hammering beat there as he attempted some sort of composure. "Sorry, you startled me. I..."

"What are you doing in my office?" she repeated.

Chapter Fourteen

When Miranda returned to her office after a long day downtown researching the history of her building, she found a man standing in front of her desk and all the folders she had brought up from the basement were scattered around the floor. She first suspected an intruder was ransacking the place, then realized it was Jay but found no relief in that fact. He was in her office and it looked like he was snooping through the papers on her desk, making no attempt at hiding the mess he was making while snooping.

"What are doing in my office?"

"I was looking for you."

"Here I am," she heard the defensive tone in her voice but didn't bother trying to call it back. "What can I do for you?" She bent to pick up the folders on the floor and start tidying them back onto her desk and he knelt to help her.

"Sorry, the cat did this. I don't know what she was doing, she just started digging and knocking everything on the floor. It was the strangest thing."

Right, the cat did it.

"Sure. Minx-the-cat did it. No problem. So...what can I do for you? Have you learned anything yet?"

"Minx? Is that the cat's name? Somehow that suits her..." he mumbled to himself. "No, I haven't found anything yet. What about you? Anything?"

He could have lied to her, men were good at that, but she sensed he was being truthful. She relaxed.

"Actually, these are some of the files from the basement. I was up reading until early this morning and decided to bring them up here where I can look at them better. My desk chair is a lot more comfortable than the floor I sat on last night." She was only half joking, the chair was a lot more comfortable, but the real reason she'd brought the folders upstairs was so she could take some notes about the details and look into them online.

"Do you think it's wise to leave them out where anyone could see them? At least until we figure out what is going on around here?" He was right, why hadn't she thought of that? Was she just tired and not thinking clearly when she carried the files upstairs?

"You may be right, I need to be more careful."

"Did you find anything of use to us in these files?"

"Not really, but I want to do some research on some of the details, go online and see what I can find. At least I have some names and dates that I can look into."

"What are you hoping to find?"

"So far, I'm just trying to get an idea of the previous owners of this building. From there, I don't know. But it's a start."

"Maybe while you are searching the previous owners you might find something about how the building was used. It might explain the layout, floor plans, and the original structure of the building before subsequent remodels and placement of walls and rooms."

"You're right again."

"What's the plan next?"

"Hmm, I don't know. I guess I'll keep reading through the files in the basement until I find something that helps. Until then, business as usual around this place."

"Speaking of the internet, have you considered installing a webcam here as another tool to reach people who might want to adopt one of the cats?"

"What do you mean?"

"I've seen it before, you have a camera in one room where the cats spend the most time. Visitors to your website could watch the cats in action. They could log in anytime of the day or night and check out the cats you have for adoption, see how they interact with other cats, that sort of thing. It would be a great way for prospective clients to get to know the cats and their personalities." Where that came from Jay didn't know. One minute they are discussing the files in the basement, then next he's volunteering to do more work? He had plenty of other jobs on his schedule, why would he commit to more work here, especially if he wasn't getting paid to do it?

"Is that something you could install?"

"Absolutely. I've done a few in a surveillance situation. You've probably heard of them, where people can check in from work and monitor their home on their phone or laptop."

"Speaking of surveillance..."

"You want some installed in other places around the business?"

"Maybe. I'll think about it."

"Still think somebody is spying on you in your office?"

"How else would you explain some of the stuff that's been happening? There's no way anyone would know that stuff unless they heard my conversations in my office. No way."

"We can install something in your office, but you have to remember that every time you are working in there you will be on camera. Would that bother you?"

"Not if I am the only one who knows about it and is monitoring what is being filmed."

"Okay then. You just say the word and I will pick up what we need and get it all installed."

"Yes, yes. I'll do that." The sound of scratching demanded her attention and she looked down to find Minx pawing at the papers on the desk beneath her, the only folder that wasn't cast on the floor.

"What do you have there?" Jay asked.

"I don't know, just one of the files I brought up from the basement," she said as she pulled the folder out from under the cat and got a look at it. "Oh, yes. It thought this was strange so I brought it up to read it better. It looks like something out of a tabloid, nothing but gossip, but since it is about the people who used to own this building I wanted to see what it had to say. The article isn't that old but it is about stuff that happened a long time ago."

"What does it say?"

"Have you ever heard of Cloris and Dodd Meriweather? Evidently they were very well known in these parts back when this building was first renovated, I get the feeling they had a lot of money. I grew up in this area and never heard of them."

"No, the names don't sound familiar to me either. What does the article have to say about them?"

"Let me see," she scanned over the article. "Looks like there was some scandal involving Cloris, that's the wife. The couple never had any children...yada yada yada...there was an affair...or at least the media is reporting an affair...oh, okay, here it is. It talks about a split and who will get the money in a divorce. I wonder why...oh, I see. That's it then, typical gossip."

"What? Is there anything about ownership of this building if there was a divorce?"

"I'm guessing it would be included in the pre-nuptial agreement, that's mostly what the article is about, the pre-nup. There's one other thing, though."

"Oh?"

"Yeah, the paper is suggesting there was a baby and that it was all covered up. Silly rich people, don't they know secrets always get them into trouble? The truth always comes out at some point."

"Back to the article, what ever happened to the couple? Did they end up getting a divorce?"

"It's not real clear but I would guess that they did. I have to wonder, though..."

"What?"

"Who saved the articles I've found and why are they preserved in that room in the basement? What's the significance of that?"

"Good question."

"I want to find out more about this couple. If this article is so important that somebody saved it, this couple must be important. I want to know who owned the building after they did and what happened to them."

"How did you acquire the building?"

"It was donated by an anonymous benefactor."

"And you said there have been anonymous deposits to your bank account?"

"Yes, do you think…"

"Exactly, your benefactor – whoever they are – is still supporting your cause. It has to be the same person."

"But what is the connection to these people?"

"Maybe nothing. I think we need to find out more."

"I'll start on the internet then go from there," Miranda said, suddenly excited about what she might find.

"And I will get back to checking behind those attic walls. But can you do me a favor?"

"Sure. What do you need?"

"Can you make sure this cat stays here with you? I'd swear the thing was stalking me and it's kinda freaking me out." Miranda felt the smirk threaten but quickly quelled it before Jay could see it.

He was serious.

Chapter Fifteen

Jay did not get back to the attic for a couple of days.

One of his other clients had a repair emergency that he had to take care of so he was working late nights getting them taken care of before wedding guests were due to arrive. The grandparents were providing housing for several family members from out of town and Jay was hired to update three rooms that would serve as bedrooms.

At some point during the end of the job, Jay mentioned the work he was doing at the *Kitty Kastle*.

"Oh, the old Meriweather place. Yes, I remember that. Boy that brings back memories..." Grant Huckabee chortled as he said it and Jay suspected there was wickedness behind the memories. The fact that the Meriweather name came up for the second time in the past few days – a name he had never heard before now – was something he refused to count as coincidence.

"You knew the Meriweathers?" Jay asked the older man.

"Nobody really *knew* the Meriweathers. Good God, no. They were in a class of their own, at least that's what they thought." So, not fond memories.

"What can you tell me about them? I ask because the new owner is curious, just wants to learn about the history of the place." Without giving anything away, Jay knew an opportunity when he saw one. He needed to get this guy to talk.

"The missus came from money, lots of money. Nobody knows where she found the guy she married but he definitely wasn't from her social class. Scuttlebutt was that he was her gardener or something, some said he blackmailed her into marrying him. It was not a love match." All this gossip from the husband, Jay would have expected it from the wife, who was just joining them from having been checking out his work.

"I simply love what you've done," the wife told Jay, interrupting her husband. "We'll have to keep you in mind when we are ready to remodel the master bedroom."

"Honey," the husband said to the wife, "I was just telling him about the Meriweathers. You remember them?" At the question, the wife scrunched up her nose in obvious distaste.

"How could I forget, I wish I could forget. What a terrible pair of people. I'm just glad those horrid people didn't bring a child into this world. Can you imagine the life that poor child would have had with parents like that?"

"Just curious, what would he have been blackmailing her with?" Jay tried to remain calm in his questioning but this was just too good! To accidentally fall into a conversation about the people he and Miranda had just discussed not three days ago.

"It's just idle gossip, mind you, but people said there was a baby."

"I thought you just said there weren't any children."

"Oh, not a child between Cloris and Dodd. They both had affairs, but one of them...it was rumored...resulted in a child."

Wasn't that what Miranda had read in one of the tabloids she found in the basement, something about a baby?

They needed to get a better look at the Meriweathers and what would have happened to the building if their marriage ended in divorce.

Better yet, what happened to the baby?

Chapter Sixteen

Miranda kept hitting a brick wall.

The farthest she could get in researching previous owners of her building was the Meriweathers and their ownership ended over twenty years ago, according to the public records. Ownership was acquired by a corporation after that, J&K Incorporated, and that's where the trail went cold.

J&K Incorporated was a mystery. No website, no listing in business or residential phone books, no record of it anywhere that she could find.

The only interesting tidbit of information she was able to verify was that the Meriweathers' marriage ended about the same time the building changed owners but Miranda still could not find anything telling her that the two things were connected in any way.

So, she was back in the basement, methodically digging through the rest of the file cabinets, trying to organize the information she found on a notebook she kept nearby. She was not looking for specific information, just recording the information she found with the intent to process it in her head later. Right now, the plan was just to narrow all the masses of information down to what was useful.

She was just about to give up for the night when she ran across a file of photographs, not the old black and white or sepia tones she would have expected, these were more recent. These portraits were taken in a studio by a professional, nothing casual or spontaneous. These were meticulously posed and orchestrated. The first picture in the folder was one of Cloris Meriweather, the first Miranda was seeing up close. Every other picture she had seen so far was in newspaper clippings from a distance or in a group.

This was the first time Miranda was seeing the woman in detail, with all her features clear enough to make out and distinguishing marks visible. There was something about the eyes, but she could not figure out what it was. Something familiar, uncanny, and unique.

It was the photo she found next that rocketed everything from simply curious to earth shattering.

Cloris Meriweather was holding a baby.

It was hard to tell if the baby picture had been taken before or after the first portrait, and Miranda was not even sure the timing was important. The fact that she was seeing the woman with the baby was proof positive, as far as Miranda was concerned, that the baby story was true. Now she needed to figure out how important that fact was when applied to the story of the building. How did a baby figure into that picture?

Then Miranda noticed a particular detail that was missing from the entire drawer full of photos; not a single photo of the husband, Dodd. Did that explain how old these photos were, some time after the divorce?

She pulled her notebook to the top of the cabinet and started a list of things she wanted to check on when she got to her computer. Marriage and divorce records for the Meriweathers, birth certificate for the baby (assuming she was able to zero in on the date the baby was born, and that was a longshot), J&K Incorporated and if the business name was ever registered in town, any other Meriweathers that might be living in town or where they disappeared to.

Quite a to-do list but important details that they needed before they could learn anything else. She doubted that she would find any copies of the records among the basement files and she was not even sure she was patient enough to look for them there. The internet or courthouse would be the fastest way to find them. Maybe. She'd soon find out.

She checked her watch and found that, again, she'd been working in the basement all night and it was after four in the morning. No wonder her neck and back were killing her and her head was throbbing. Pushing herself up from the chair she'd dragged down there from her office, Miranda walked around the well lit room to stretch her body and shake out the kinks. As she walked around the perimeter of the room, something at the back of the room drew her in, ridges in the concrete wall near the floor. It was no wonder she'd never noticed it before now, she had been focusing on the stuff in the file cabinets not the actual walls surrounding them.

Somebody had scratched something in to the surface of the block wall of the foundation. Miranda didn't know much about building construction but it looked like the wall had been coated in some form of epoxy, probably what was sealing the room and keeping it airtight and controlling moisture from getting in. In that epoxy coating was where she found what she wasn't finding in the file cabinet drawers; a name, date and clue.

March 1, 1982
My Precious Baby Boy
I Love you
Please forgive me

Exactly what she had been hoping for! A birth date for the baby Cloris was rumored to have given birth to. The only thing Miranda did not have was anything telling her what ever happened to the baby.

Now she had a date to check, though, and if the baby's information was scratched into this wall, it was a safe bet he was born in this city. Miranda should be able to find a birth certificate.

Quickly jotting down the information from the wall, Miranda tucked her notebook under her arm, closed the file cabinet drawer she'd been working on, and shut off all the lights as she headed upstairs.

She could not wait to tell Jay what she'd found.

Now they were getting somewhere.

Chapter Seventeen

It took him long enough to get there but Jay was finally looking at what had been driving him crazy for days, if not weeks. He was on the fourth floor of Miranda's building staring blindly into the gaping hole in the wall that started out the size of his hand and was now the size of a chest high doorway. That doorway was what served him well as he ducked and stepped through it to see mysteries that had previously been hidden from him…and the black cat who followed him into the darkness.

He found a room that was more of a passageway than a room. As he followed it, flashlight in hand and black cat in the lead, he found that the passageway wound its way around the outside of the fourth floor. He had to bend over to fit because of the slant of the roof, but he could still walk all the way around until he ended up back where he started. The passage was empty of anything suggesting the presence of somebody but he knew its existence confirmed that it was built for somebody to get around in, maybe without the occupants of the inner rooms knowing it.

Then it hit him.

Was there something like this on all levels of the building? On the first floor surrounding Miranda's office, maybe? And, if so, were they all connected to each other by some hidden doorways or staircases that would take a person from level to level without having to leave the secrecy to venture to the inner elevator and staircase?

The fourth floor was currently unoccupied so a person could walk around without being seen any time of the day…or could they? Had he not heard what he thought was somebody walking around the other day when he thought it was Wade?

"Meow." As crazy as it sounded to him in his head, he and the cat suddenly seemed to understand each other, like the cat was reading his mind.

"Cat. Do you know where the passageway is on the third floor?"

"Meow."

"I'll take that as a yes. There's some fancy kibble in it for you if you can show me where it is."

"Meow." The cat walked up to Jay and started rubbing in and around his legs and Jay took that as an invitation to pick her up in his arms. He was rewarded with a steady rumbling purr and the butting of her head against the bottom of his chin and he suddenly questioned why he had ever thought he did not like cats. Who wouldn't like the trust and affection he was feeling from the cat in his arms?

"Okay, Cat. Let's go see what you can show me on the third floor." Miranda's apartment, the only residential area of the building. Would she mind if he were to snoop around there? She said he had free run of the place while he was still working there. He didn't want to alert her to anything until he had something to show her, so this he'd have to do alone. It was the middle of the day, her normal working hours. She was either working down in the shelter or in her office.

He quickly took the stairs down one level and let himself into the third floor apartment. All he had to do was scope out the wall placements and knock on a few walls at different places and he would have his answers.

After entering the apartment the cat struggled and Jay set her on the floor, where she immediately took off and disappeared into Miranda's bedroom. Something made Jay follow the cat, ignoring the pangs of guilt for invading Miranda's private space, especially her bedroom.

He had not been in the room since she moved in. He had only been in the completed apartment the day he was checking out her wiring, so he was seeing her living conditions for the first time. What he saw did not surprise him, she was a neat freak. It was what he did *not* see that surprised him, she had very few personal belongings to make a mess with: The bed, a chair that served as a side table and some clear plastic storage bins against one wall that held what looked like neatly folded stacks of clothing. She had very little clothing. What woman had this little clothing? He had installed a large walk-in closet when he built this apartment for her but it stood empty. Why did she store her meager supply of clothing in plastic bins, as though everything was temporary and she was ready to move at any given moment? What did he really know about her life and her background? Nothing.

"Meow."

Back to his original reason for begin there. The cat called to him from the walk-in closet and he followed the command and joined her there.

"Meow."

"What, Cat?" Jay didn't see anything unusual about the room but reached for the light switch to get a better look. "What am I looking for...and why am I asking a cat?" he muttered to himself as he started examining the walls around him, looking for anything that might suggest a passageway or alteration to the walls he'd installed. Working his way from one side of the closet, top to bottom, to the corner and then to the next wall, he saw nothing different.

He worked his way to the back wall, about to move on to the last wall behind him, when he saw it.

A crack, or seam, opened in the corner joining the two walls. When he'd finished the room that wall was perfectly taped and mudded, the work of his hired drywallers had passed his own strict inspection. There was no way that crack was there when he approved the work only two months ago.

The cat sat silent as Jay examined the walls, only making a move when Jay walked from one corner of the room to the opposite of the same wall, finding a matching crack running the entire length of the wall from top to bottom.

Motivated by hunch only, Jay went to the center of the wall, placed the palms of both hands flat against the wall, and shoved.

The wall moved easily backward, as though it was a solid panel meant to move as one piece and not connect to the surrounding walls. Exactly what it was, a stand alone wall that had been built to fit snug into place as the back wall of the closet, serving as an entrance to the passageway hidden behind it.

How was it possible for there to be a hidden passageway behind these walls without Jay knowing about it? He had personally built the walls for the apartment, the walls for this room. Where...how...when...who moved *those* walls and replaced them with *these* walls?

Pushing the wall aside so he could step inside the hidden room behind it, Jay pulled his flashlight from the pocket of his tool belt and ventured inside. He was mystified and a little angry at what he was finding.

Months of planning, measuring, building, constructing, and finishing had gone into building this apartment for Miranda and he was finding that each wall he'd built had been moved. He could see the evidence of that on the bare wood floors the beam of his flashlight was illuminating for him. Without measuring, he guessed the walls had been moved at least four feet in from his original placement. That would take somebody skilled at carpentry, drywall, and mechanicals to be able to do that and they had to have been able to do it quickly without Jay and his team ever noticing the changes. How was that possible and when was it done, at what stage of the construction had it happened? This was the only floor of the building that had new exterior walls, on the other three levels they had worked with the walls as they were, only building and relocating walls located at the center of the building.

He'd focus on the details later, right now he wanted to see where the passageway would take him and what – or who – he would find there.

Chapter Eighteen

"I don't know, I just don't know," Miranda said as she sat at her desk with Kaye, looking at the documents spread out on the desktop before them.

"Come on, why are you pursuing this? It's interesting, sure, but don't you think you're getting a little carried away with all this?"

"I don't know. It's just a gut feeling, something weird is going on around here," Miranda insisted.

"But what does all this have to do with it? And where did you find all this stuff?"

Kaye did not know about the room in the basement, nor did she know about the strange noises Miranda had been hearing at night around her apartment upstairs. Miranda had stopped sharing information with Kaye since her suspicions about the massage bed. She still didn't know how that private conversation in her office had landed them the mysterious gift. She didn't suspect Kaye of anything malicious, she just wanted to figure out what was going on around the place without having to explain herself to anybody but Jay. How had she suddenly grown so close to Jay in such a short time? Up until six months ago Jay had been a stranger to her, she had never met him and never heard of him, but now he was her one and only confidant, the only person she trusted with these secrets. Kaye used to be that person, the person with whom Miranda shared *everything*.

"I'm just curious about the history of the building, that's all. What do we really know about this building, how old it is, who were its previous owners, and who donated it to us? Aren't you the least bit curious?" Miranda asked.

"Not really. I am just very grateful to the person – or persons – who donated it and wanted to remain anonymous. I think we need to respect their privacy." With Kaye's last words she dropped her eyes and turned away from Miranda, a move that suddenly made Miranda suspicious. It was a classic avoidance move; she was hiding something.

"How can you not be even a little bit curious?"

"I don't know, I'm just not." Again she avoided eye contact with Miranda.

"Kaye." Miranda watched as Kaye walked away from her, absently running her fingers along the books lined up on the bookshelves as she moved toward the door. "Kaye. How long have we been friends?" Kaye stopped and slowly turned to face her.

"What?"

"How long have we been friends?"

"I don't know. Why?" Miranda had obviously surprised her with the question.

"Just answer the question. How long would you say that we have been friends?"

"At least ten years, when you first started the shelter. Remember? I was your first volunteer. Yeah, over ten years ago."

"It was actually twelve years ago. You worked at the bank where I went for a loan to open the shelter. They denied me the loan."

"Okay. You're probably right." Kaye started to turn away from her again but Miranda stopped her with her next question.

"I always wondered how you found me and ended up at the shelter back then, I never could figure out why you would quit such a good job working at a bank and come to work for me as a volunteer." The more Miranda thought about it, the more she wondered at their unlikely friendship. "Why did you do that, how could you afford to do that?"

"I don't know what you are talking about. Now...enough about this, I think we both have work to do. I think I heard somebody calling me from the other room…"

"Kaye," Miranda hurried to block Kaye's escape. "What is going on? What are you keeping from me? We have been friends for over ten years, remember? Why won't you answer my questions?" Miranda saw the pain wash over the other woman's face, she was fighting an inner battle, struggling to maintain a stronghold on secrets Miranda was desperate to unleash. "Please, Kaye. Tell me!"

"I can't! You don't understand! I *can't* tell you! It would ruin everything!" Kaye shoved Miranda out of her way and hurried from the room, leaving Miranda more confused and frustrated than she had been in days.

"Kaye!" she called after the other woman but it was too late, Kaye disappeared down the hall and the sound of the back door slamming told Miranda she'd left the building.

What just happened?

How had the moment deteriorated so quickly from a simple question to the point where Kaye was desperately running away in tears?

What just happened?

Chapter Nineteen

An empty passageway but a passageway just the same, that was what Jay found behind the wall in Miranda's closet. He followed the tight room all the way around. It encircled the entire building, surrounding the third floor in a protective five foot wide chamber, cleverly angling the space to give the illusion that her windows were snug to the outside of the building so she had no clue that her walls were five feet in from the actual exterior walls of the building. Even though he found the passageway, Jay was no closer to discovering the reason for its existence or who had put it there. He let himself out of Miranda's apartment after carefully replacing the wall in her closet then took the main staircase to the first floor.

It was time to tell Miranda what he had found...or had not found.

Maybe she had been luckier and found some information they could use.

He found Miranda in her office, crumpled over her desk crying.

He cleared his throat then lightly knocked on the open door to get her attention before entering. There was nothing he hated more than a crying woman, but at least this time he was pretty sure he wasn't the one who had caused the crying.

"Miranda?" He watched as she quickly sat up, wiping the tears from her face and squaring her shoulders to put on a brave face. If he had not seen her crying he could almost believe the facade she presented, but he'd already seen the tears and felt the awkwardness that came with them. "Do you have a minute?"

"Sure, sure." After swiping one last time at the tears, she sniffled and faced him. "What can I do for you?"

"Is this a bad time?"

"No, come on in and sit down. Tell me what you've found...if you've found something." The hopeful tone in her voice made him wish he had more to tell her. Maybe it would be enough. He shut the door behind him and picked a chair facing her to sit in.

"I don't know how much help this is, but I have found something. I had to rip a hole in the wall on the fourth floor but it was worth it, and I will repair it as soon as possible. Don't worry."

"What did you find?"

"Just as I expected but couldn't believe until I actually saw it. There are passageways, or what seem to be passageways, around the perimeter of the building. I found them on the third floor, too."

"You were in my apartment?" She didn't seem upset by the fact, just curious, so he continued.

"As I was saying, I found passageways that go all the way around the building on both floors. They were professionally built by somebody who knew what they were doing - a carpenter or somebody skilled in carpentry and millwork - and they were able to work fast. It looks like they relocated the walls I built, and that could not have been an easy task. Not only that, there is no evidence that they have been altered. To get those walls moved in from the original location they had to have cut and replastered every seam without me being able to detect it. We must have come in each day and continued our work, oblivious to the fact that the rooms and walls had been relocated. It's the strangest thing I've ever seen."

"If they are on those two floors, do you think we'll find them on the remaining floors? This floor?" She was asking if there were passageways behind the walls of her office. She didn't need to utter the words, he was wondering the same thing. She dropped her voice to a whisper, "Do you think there's somebody wandering around behind those walls, maybe spying on me...on us?"

"I can't think why but it's entirely possible." At this point, Jay would believe anything about this building. It was beginning to resemble a carnival funhouse for all the weird things it revealed to him each day.

"How do we know if there is somebody there, can you tell if there is a secret passageway behind one of these walls right now?"

"I built these bookcases. I measured, nailed, trimmed, and installed them on each wall in here. I can not imagine how I could have missed that there was something odd about the walls I was working on, but until today I would have thought that about your apartment walls, too. This is just crazy."

"Crazy, yeah. But..."

"Yeah, I know. I know what I found." Needing to change the subject for a minute, he focused on something else. "Have you learned anything from the papers you've been looking over?"

"Yes and no. What I have found is mostly newspaper clippings and the subject matter seems to be focused on the same thing, but it does not tell me anything useful. Whoever was saving all those files in the basement, and had the basement room built in the first place, had a personal agenda and it was a very focused agenda. Maybe just information about people they knew or people they were related to, nothing tells me any more than that."

"Hmm, maybe we just need to look at it from a different point of view. What did you find that was specifically about this building? And the Meriweathers?"

"Actually, it's all starting to give me a headache. Can you show me the passageways? I want to see what has been hiding behind the walls of my apartment."

"Okay. Now?"

"Yes, now."

Chapter Twenty

Miranda was not ready to tell Jay about her strange conversation with Kaye, she was still trying to wrap her head around it. She had not lied when she said she was getting a headache. She hoped the walk away from her office would help, anything to get away from the stack of papers on her desk and the memories of Kaye's strange behavior.

Before she and Kaye had started the path down the blowup, they had been looking at the bank statement and the latest deposit of money showing up there. Another twenty thousand, deposited two days ago. Anonymous was what the bank manager told her over the phone, just like the others.

The account was growing ever closer to reaching one hundred thousand dollars!

Who in the world had that kind of money to keep giving away, especially to a shelter for cats, and only cats? She almost felt guilty that all that money wasn't being spread around to help save more needy creatures, but she wasn't about to turn it down now. The shelter had a lot of expenses that money could cover, with cash left over for future needs and expenses. One hundred thousand dollars!

Miranda started to bring up the subject of things she had been looking into regarding the history of the building, its previous owners, and the possible connection to where the money might be coming from and that was when Kaye started her near meltdown.

Miranda hadn't noticed Kaye going through any stress recently, was she that bad a friend that she hadn't noticed her best friend in some kind of emotional trouble? Kaye had always been the strong one in their friendship, always the one who could calm Miranda when things got rough. Kaye was the one who convinced Miranda to walk away from the abusive ex husband and make a clean break – the best thing she could have done, thanks to Kaye – but now Miranda seemed to be the one remaining calm. A calm she did not know how to deal with nor did she trust it to last long.

It was the night after Jay revealed the secret passageway around her third floor apartment and she was spending the night in her office at her desk, her head resting on her desk in exhaustion. Now that she knew of the passageway, there was no way she could sleep in that apartment. It was like living in a fishbowl. Her privacy had been violated, she felt exposed, insecure, and vulnerable.

The room was lit only by the small lamp on her desk, the hallways outside her open door were dark. She heard an occasional scuffling of what she assumed were kitties doing their usual nocturnal wanderings around the place, but other than that it was quiet. Too quiet. Unnervingly quiet. She suddenly wished she was tucked safely in her bed where, up until this afternoon, she felt safe from the world. Now she no longer felt like she had a safe place.

Then the noises began.

She quickly clicked off her desk lamp and slid off her chair, curling up under the desk to listen.

It was the footsteps she heard first, just like those she thought she'd imagined before. Now she knew they were real. The sounds were coming from behind the walls of her office. The loud scraping sounds, much like a large piece of furniture being moved, and then the footsteps were right there in her office. Two sets of footsteps, walking in front of her desk and stopping.

"Shh, I'm not sure where she is. Probably in bed by now. It's well after midnight and she hasn't been sleeping well so she's due to collapse from exhaustion." Hushed tones, Miranda could barely make out what they were saying.

"Poor thing. I hate not being able to tell her anything."

"It's for her own good, and his."

"But she's starting to suspect things." Was that Kaye's voice? "She's been looking through those papers of yours, they found the archives in the basement. She doesn't know that I know, but I do."

Yes! It was Kaye! But who was she talking to and who were they talking about? Were they talking about her? Miranda tucked her legs in tighter to her body and buried her face in her knees so they would not hear her breathe.

"What has she discovered?"

"I don't know, I wouldn't listen. I tried to discourage her from digging too deep."

"It will be okay, trust me. Even if she finds anything important, it won't make sense to her. There are just too many details and I have made sure to keep the details under wraps. She will never know unless one of us tells her. Trust me, Kaye. Everything will be okay."

"Okay. I trust you."

"Now, let's go see all my babies. I've missed them so!"

Miranda heard them leave the room but she stayed tucked under the desk, afraid to move or be discovered. She ignored the logic that tried to convince her that this was her home, her office, her place of business and that she did not need to hide from anybody. She ignored the fact that *they* were actually trespassers and that one or both of them were lying to her, keeping secrets, and betraying her by keeping those secrets. All she wanted to think about was that she could not let them know that she was there, hiding under the desk, and that she heard their conversation and the implications of what she'd heard.

What was Kaye up to? Who was that other person? Should she confront Kaye at the first chance she got or should she pretend she did not know anything and try to catch her in a lie or stake the place out at night and try to catch the two people, see what they were up to?

Would she be able to pretend she had not heard Kaye?

But then…what had she actually heard? That was the real question.

She needed to tell Jay, as soon as possible. Maybe he would know what to do.

Miranda stayed tucked under the desk until daylight started to filter in through the window blinds and the footsteps disappeared behind the wall. Another night with no sleep if Jay decided that they would need to stake out the place tonight.

Maybe she could catch a good nap sometime during the day.

Chapter Twenty One

Jay completed all the scheduled repairs at the *Kitty Kastle* but was in no any hurry to wrap up and move on to his other contracted jobs, something held him in place and would not let him walk away. Perhaps it was the woman sitting behind the desk looking at him like he had all the answers in the world. He didn't, but it was a good feeling to have somebody believe in him. He felt like a hero yet didn't know why.

"Tell me again what you saw and heard," he said and Miranda repeated the story almost exactly as she had told him the first time.

"I'm positive one of the people talking was Kaye."

"Could you tell where the scraping sound came from? If it really was one of these walls maybe we can find it and look behind it."

"I couldn't tell from under the desk. I just know it wasn't this wall over here," she pointed to the wall behind the desk, "I would have seen them from there. That only leaves one wall. Besides...if it is like the passageways on the other floors, don't you think it would be the exterior wall?"

"Good point." Jay walked to the wall in question and started running his hand over the wall between the shelves mounted there, knocking lightly hoping to hear some inconsistencies in the depth of the wall. It still bothered him that he had not noticed anything when he was building the bookcases. The project took him several weeks to complete but still he was oblivious to anything weird about the walls. The bookshelves were mounted to the wall rather than a shelf back, giving him the ability to knock directly on the surface of the wall and not on a wood backing of a bookcase.

His knocks paid off.

There it was, a hollow spot behind the wall.

"I think I found something here," he said to Miranda and was rewarded with one of those hero worship looks he was growing very fond of. She rushed to his side and leaned in close to his side, trying to get a better look. He knocked lightly on the hollow spot. "Hear that? That is a void zone in the wall that should not be there. Here, listen to the difference when I hit a solid zone over here." He demonstrated the difference then knocked again on the hollow spot. She nodded and he felt the zing of her anxious energy.

"So, what do we do now?" she asked.

"How about we have a talk?" they were interrupted by a voice at the door.

Jay and Miranda turned to find Kaye standing in the open doorway with an older woman smiling beside her. "I think it's time we talked." Kaye directed the woman to a seat near Miranda's sitting area then took a chair beside her.

Chapter Twenty Two

Jay and Miranda each pulled up chairs facing Kaye and sat back silently, waiting for Kaye to start the conversation.

"You're probably wondering who I am," the stranger in the room spoke, a smile softening her face and her eyes wandering over Jay with an interest that would have been creepy if Miranda hadn't detected a familiarity in the face that she couldn't immediately put her finger on. "My name is Cloris Meriweather, I think you are familiar with the name." She turned her smile briefly on Miranda then swept back to Jay, who started to squirm under the scrutiny.

Then Miranda saw it, the face she had been studying for several days, the woman who had remained a mystery yet demanded that her story be heard. This woman previously owned the building and she was the person Miranda suspected had installed and filled the secret room in the basement. If she was responsible for that room, did she have anything to do with the passageways?

"Did you used to live in this building?" Miranda surprised herself with the question.

"No. I can honestly say that I didn't *use to* live in this building." Why did Miranda feel like it was a trick answer?

"But you are a previous owner...right?"

"Yes. That is true. I used to own this building." Miranda still felt like the woman was being evasive with her answers, especially since her eyes were still on Jay as she spoke. Then the woman turned and Miranda got her first look at the woman's eyes. Familiar eyes.

Miranda quickly looked at Jay, then back at the woman who called herself Cloris Meriweather. The woman nodded at the question she must have seen on Miranda's face.

"Are you…?" Miranda whispered.

Again, the nod.

"What?" Jay asked, impatience in his tone. Miranda reached out and caught his hand, squeezing it tight in hers. He turned his curious gaze on her, eyebrows raised in silent question and she turned back to look at Cloris Meriweather.

"Jay is your son…isn't he?" A nod was her answer. "You gave him up for adoption when he was born." A statement, not a question.

"Yes," Cloris said. "It was the only way to keep him safe." Miranda felt Jay's hand tighten in hers but he didn't pull away, his eyes were fully locked on Cloris now.

"And, Kaye? What is your part in everything?" Miranda asked her friend.

"I am her daughter and personal assistant. Jay is my half brother." Jay's hand tightened painfully on hers then went to pull away and Miranda wrapped her other hand around it to keep it in place.

"So…?"

"I think it's time to stop keeping secrets, Mother. They deserve to know the truth," Kaye said.

"Yes. Yes, you're right," Cloris said to Jay and the two looked at each other as though there was nobody else in the room.

"First, I want to know. Where is Dodd?" Why this was her first question, Miranda didn't know but suddenly it was important to know.

"He's dead. Has been for over twenty years."

"Miserable piece of--" Kaye tried to say but was quickly shushed by her mother.

"Hush, darling. He was your father."

"No, he wasn't. He was only the violent bearer of sperm that created me…not my father."

"How did he die?" Miranda persisted. Kaye and Cloris exchanged a long look before turning back to Miranda.

"Why…I killed him, of course," Cloris said with no emotion, just as a matter of fact.

Chapter Twenty Three

All it took was a quick lookup on the internet to find that Cloris hadn't really killed her husband. If the woman would have had internet at her disposal in the past twenty years, she could have easily found that her husband actually died in a car accident. Not her fault. A massive heart attack and he lost control of the car, he died instantly.

"But I thought…" Cloris gasped, her hand at her throat. "All these years, wasted." A lone tear escaped and ran down her face.

"Wait a minute, I still don't understand. What does any of this have to do with…everything?" Jay asked.

"I think I know," Miranda said and everything was starting to become clear. "You thought you killed your husband. That's why you have been hiding here all these years, isn't it?" Cloris nodded.

"But you didn't, but...you were *planning* to kill him weren't you?" Again, she nodded.

"He was a monster," Kaye interjected. "When Mother discovered she was pregnant, Dodd blackmailed her boyfriend and he ended up taking his own life. Mother was forced to marry Dodd. She gave you up," Kaye looked at Jay, "because she knew Dodd hated you and that your life would be in danger if she ever let Dodd get near you. I was just an accident."

"A very happy and joyous accident, my darling," Cloris said.

"If you call being conceived through rape, happy and joyous..."

"But how did you end up here?" Miranda still didn't have all the answers, and Jay appeared to be in shock.

"She had everything in place to get rid of him. She set up the properties in the corporation name, put everything else in my name. Everything she needed to do to disappear without the government taking it away."

"Wait a minute…properties…plural?"

"Let's take a walk…" Kaye helped her mother from her chair. Jay rose with Miranda still gripping his hand in hers.

"Where are we going?" Jay asked.

"Next door, the building next door."

"You own the other buildings?" Jay asked.

"No, you and your sister do. All the buildings on this block. And it's time you check out your property," Cloris said with a little sass in her amazingly strong voice. She led them toward the bookcases and Kaye reached for the hidden switch that exposed the hidden passageway then motioned them inside.

"Of course you would have a hidden way to travel between buildings. Why not. You've been hiding in this building so long without being detected…" Jay said, sarcasm dripping from his voice.

"No, darling. I haven't been living in this building all these years. I've been living next door."

What they found next door was a luxurious palace, furnished in the best of everything. Undetectable from the outside, Cloris had designed the inside of this building for somebody to live a very good life.

"Are all the buildings connected like this one?"

"Of course."

"And, Kaye? I'm guessing you live here as well? All this time, you've been living right next door?" A nod.

"I guess I don't have to ask *why*. You thought you were hiding from the law for having murdered your husband," Miranda was still asking the questions, she guessed Jay was still dealing with the shock. A nod, then a sheepish smile was the answer she got from Cloris. "But I would like to know…oh. Is this about me?" Another nod.

"And Jay," Kaye said. Miranda didn't know there was a *her-and-Jay* thing, but now it was starting to grow on her.

"And the kitties, of course," Cloris said. "And that's how it all began. That day you walked into my bank and applied for a loan. I had to turn you down because I wanted to be more involved without the bank…this way works much better." A smile wrapped up the story.

"There's one more thing," Cloris said and even Kaye seemed surprised this time. "Jay, I have something to show you."

It took a long walk through the underground tunnels again then they were on ground floor on what Miranda suspected was the third building down from the *Kitty Kastle*.

"I hope you don't mind, but I had this one made up for you. There's still a lot to be done, I know you prefer building for yourself, but the basics are there for you to customize as you like." Cloris seemed anxious for Jay to approve but he was still not saying anything.

"I've hated you my whole life," Jay spat between gritted teeth and a rigid jaw. "Now you come back into my life after having been there without my knowing it, and I'm supposed to be happy because you gave me a building? How does that make up for everything?" What Miranda had thought was shock had obviously been anger boiling beneath the surface.

"I understand, darling. All I ask is to give it time. Believe me, everything I did was to protect you," Cloris said then nodded to Kaye who picked up a wooden box and handed it to Jay. The box was made of dark walnut and covered with intricate carvings from top to bottom, a heavy lock was mounted on the front. "Please take this. I believe you have the key to unlock it."

Miranda watched as Jay reached into his pocket and pulled out a skeleton key. He held it briefly before him, dangling it from a red ribbon, then stuffed it back into his pocket. He turned and walked away, back to the tunnels that would take him out of there, the box tightly gripped under one arm.

Chapter Twenty Four

When Miranda returned to her office, after leaving Kaye and Cloris back at the second building, it was to find Jay sitting in her office waiting for her. The box sat open on her desk in front of him.

"There are letters. They are dated back to when I was born." The anguish in his voice hit her square in the chest and she rushed toward him, wrapping her arms around him and squeezing him tight. "She wrote me every day, explaining why she did what she did and begging for my forgiveness." He choked on the last word but she could tell he refused to let himself shed any tears.

"She loved you. She wanted to protect you."

"Yes. All these years…all these years."

"You have to forgive her. This is your chance to get to know her. Can you imagine how difficult it must have been for her…?" Miranda knew it wasn't her place to get involved, this was a family affair and she wasn't part of the family.

"Yes, of course. It's all just too much right now. I can't do it alone."

"You have your mother and your sister, your family, you won't be alone."

"Yes. But I need you."

"Yes. I'm right here, and I'm not going anywhere." Miranda placed a light kiss on his forehead without thinking then suddenly pulled back. Her eyes locked on his for a moment then his lips were on hers.

For the first time in many years, Miranda realized what it was like to be home.